Love At First Puck

Van Cole

Published by Van Cole, 2023.

LOVE AT FIRST PUCK

First edition. May 23, 2023.

Copyright © 2023 Van Cole.

ISBN: 979-8215788202

Written by Van Cole.

Table of Contents

Love At First Puck
Gay First Time Romance

By: Van Cole

Foreword

All Scott has wanted since a child was to represent his favorite hockey team, but after a couple of seasons toiling away as a second string he's traded away unceremoniously. At first it hurts, but he vows to play well enough to make them regret ever letting him go.

He's welcomed at his new team by Mark, the personal trainer, and the two of them form an instant bond. Scott is unable to deny the attraction he feels, even though exploring it could jeopardize his standing among his new team-mates. Mark is an anchor to Scott, until everything around him starts to sink.

Scott is forced to ask himself if his career is more important than his personal life. He's already lost one dream, can he afford to lose another? And when it comes time to face his former club, will he prove them right or wrong?

Love At First Puck

Chapter 1

Scott walked into the general manager's office with a sense of pride. He'd been toiling away in the reserves for a couple of seasons now, and he was sure that finally he was going to be given his big break. As he approached the office he looked around at the pictures and trophies, gazing in awe at the other players who were holding their hockey sticks aloft in triumph. That's all he'd ever wanted since he was little and finally he was on the cusp of achieving it.

When he was younger he sat in the stands cheering the team to glory, and his dream had been to one day become a part of that team and lift the trophy himself. It hadn't been easy, but all the years of sacrifice were soon going to be worth it.

Scott knocked on the door of Willy Bingham's office. Scott had a wide smile on his face and thought back to his last few performances in training. He'd been putting in extra work, and it was clearly counting. He was still a young guy, having just turned 20, but a hockey player's career was a short one, and he was eager for his to begin in earnest.

A few moments later, the door opened, and Willy showed him in. Willy was a lean man, but had a fierce demeanor about him that reminded Scott of a dragon. Scott was taller, with broader shoulders, but he wouldn't have dared gone up against Willy. Neither would the rest of the players.

Willy's face was red and he almost slammed the palms of his hands down on his desk as he sat down. He took a moment to compose himself, then took a deep breath and looked at Scott.

"How're you doing Scotty?" he asked.

"Oh, I'm just fine, I'm feeling good, I'm feeling ready to play my part this season," Scott replied, hoping that he wasn't overstepping his marks. But if he knew one thing in this sport it was that confidence mattered. In order to be on that rink you have to believe that you belonged there. Hockey wasn't a game for the faint of heart, and Scott had seen too many talented players be swept away because they didn't have the mental fortitude to succeed.

Willy's face fell.

"That's good son, that's good," he said, then leaned forward and clasped his hands together. "I wanted to bring you in here today for a little chat. What are your thoughts about your career?"

"Well, I mean, I hope to be playing soon," Scott said, suddenly wondering if this was going to be the time when his career would take off after all. "I've been paying my dues and I like to think that my performances in the reserves speak for themselves. I think I'm ready to make the step up. No, I know I'm ready. Wherever and whenever you need me, I'll make you proud."

A faint smile crossed Willy's mouth.

"And what if I'm not quite ready to use you yet?" Willy asked.

"Then I guess I'll wait," Scott said forlornly.

"How long would you wait?"

Scott inhaled sharply. "However long it takes. The only thing I've ever wanted was to wear that shirt," he pointed to a shirt of one of the legendary players that hung on the wall of Willy's office. "I'll wait however long it takes to make that dream a reality."

"You know son, there's a difference between a dream and reality. Dreams never work out how you want them to. Your career is important, and you're at the age now where you have to start making decisions about what you really want out of this. You're a good kid, and you've got talent, but I'm not sure you've got what it takes to make it here."

Scott couldn't believe his ears. The world went silent for a few moments and a wave of nausea swept through him. He gripped the arms of his chair tightly as the world lurched. When he didn't reply, Willy continued to talk.

"I think that you've showed promise in your time here, but right now I have a settled squad and I'm overloaded in your position. What a player like you needs is game time, and right now I can't give you that. I'm not sure I'm going to be able to. And that's a hell of a shame, because I know how much this means to you."

"I can prove you wrong. I can train harder, I can play better, I can earn a chance!" Scott blurted out, tears stinging his eyes.

"You can try if you want to, but I'm just saying that it's not likely to happen. I've got experienced players in your position, players I trust, players who haven't let me down. If you stay here then you're going to be rotting in the reserves, and you won't develop as you should. Trust me, it's in your best interests to play, even if it's not for this team."

Scott swallowed a lump in his throat and nodded numbly.

"We've been in negotiations with another team. As I'm sure you're aware we're in need of a backup goalie, so we've arranged a trade. They've been watching you. They've had scouts coming here and they've liked what they've seen. It's a good set up, I think you'll be welcome, and I think it's in your best interest to take it."

"Do I have a choice?" Scott asked. The steely, silent gaze with which Willy responded told Scott all he needed to know. Scott pressed his lips together and nodded again.

"Then I guess I'll be off."

"This is a good thing son, trust me. It'll be the making of you. You'll get a chance there that you never would have gotten here."

Deep down, Scott believed him, but it didn't make the pain hurt any less.

Chapter 2

Scott was sitting in darkness when he heard a knock at the door. Dazed, he staggered across his apartment and opened it.

"Where the hell have you been? I've been trying to ring you for hours," Steve said. He looked furious, but his face soon softened when he saw how distraught Scott was. Scott shrugged and shuffled back into the darkness of his apartment, sinking into the couch.

Steve moved after him, the bright light from the corridor being suddenly blocked.

"What's going on?" Steve asked, concern creeping into his voice.

"The worst thing ever has happened," Scott groaned.

"Oh my God, is your mom alright?"

"What? Yeah, she's fine."

"Oh, man, I thought you were going to tell me she died."

"No, it's nothing like that. I've been traded away. I'm no longer going to be a proud member of this hockey team. I'm unwanted. All the years of trying are for nothing. They don't want me. They don't think I'm good enough."

"Oh damn, did they actually say that?" Steve asked, putting his arm around Scott's shoulder, kissing him on the head. Scott barely registered the gesture, for he was utterly swallowed up by the despair churning in his gut.

"Yeah, and more. I just...all I've ever wanted is to wear that jersey. I would have waited. Maybe I can go back there again and tell them that. If they knew that I would be willing to do anything they might-"

"They already know," Steve said softly. Scott sighed and hung his head. He was finding it difficult to swallow.

"It doesn't seem like there's any point to it all now," Scott said.

"Of course there is." Steve took Scott's hands and held them tightly. "Look, I know that you've only ever wanted to play for them, but this is your career. You're amazing, and you deserve to be out there on that rink every game. It's not right for you to have to wait. You need to go out there and show them that they made a mistake in letting you go. Play your heart out, and then one day you can come back, the prodigal son, the returning hero, the champion, and then you can dictate your own terms."

Scott smiled. It was a nice thought, a pleasant fantasy, but it didn't do much to help him in his current situation. Envisioning his future seemed like a waste of time now, since the vision he'd already had was now shattered beyond repair.

"Maybe," was all he could muster. Steve sensed his anguish, and tried to move the conversation on.

"Where are the sending you?"

"I don't even know. Coach told me, but I wasn't really paying attention. Some small team down south, they're new I think. They must be desperate," Scott grinned sadly.

"Hey, come on, don't say that."

"No, it's true. Do you ever think that sometimes you've been kidding yourself? That you're not actually as good as you think you are? I've been doing this for years now, playing hockey every day, taking down notes about the opposition and my own performances, researching, learning, training, and where has it gotten me? What kind of life is this?"

"Scott, you're selling yourself short. You've worked hard and yeah, okay, you're not where you want to be. But sometimes life throws you off course and what's important is how you respond. You can only worry about what you can control, and sadly you can't control the people who want to trade you away. That's their decision, their choice, but you have choices too."

"Really? Because right now it doesn't feel like it. It feels like I'm a slave, being traded away. Maybe I should appeal, maybe there should be a revolution. There needs to be more loyalty shown from teams to their players. I bet if the situations were reversed they'd be in uproar, telling me how much money they had poured into my development, how many hours they had spent on my training. But no, they don't owe me anything. They can just decide to toss me away and uproot my life whenever they see fit. They can sit me down and tell me to my face that I'm not wanted anymore."

"Maybe they are doing you a favor, in a way. They're on fire at the moment. You wouldn't have got into the team right now. Better you move now and get on with your career rather than continue to stay in the reserves, waiting for an opportunity that's never going to come, until you're in your mid-20s and they're finally deciding to release you, but no other clubs are interested because they have no idea who you are."

"That's pretty much what coach implied. But you don't understand..."

"I do Scott, trust me, I do, and I wish that I could make this better. I wish that I could march in there and demand that they keep you and put you on the team, but I can't. They've made their decision, and now you have to make yours. You can either sit here and wallow in misery, let the world be against you and crumble, or you can stand up, square your shoulders, and make the best of it. This new team wants you. Be thankful for that. Sometimes you've gotta take one step back to take two forward. You don't know what's going to happen, but at least you'll be playing. This doesn't have to be a move that lasts forever, but you have to put everything into it, otherwise you'll blow it. And I know you're not that type of person Scott. I wouldn't be dating you if you were. I know it's a blow right now, but try and see this as an opportunity to broaden your horizons."

Scott listened to everything Steve had to say, but his head was still bowed. It was difficult to see any light at the end of the tunnel.

"I just need some time," Scott said.

"I know," Steve said. "You are going, aren't you?"

"I don't really have a choice, not if I want to keep playing hockey. But it also means something else...what's going to happen to us?"

Steve's grip on Scott's hand loosened and he sat back, exhaling deeply. Scott didn't look up at him. This was the other moment he had been dreading. His heart thumped in his chest, almost ready to break.

"Well, how far away is this place?"

"Far enough for it to matter," Scott said.

"I mean, do you want to try long distance?"

"I have no idea. I've never heard of it working well..."

"But maybe we could be the first?" Steve said. This time Scott did raise his head to look at him. Even in the darkness Scott could see the cheerful lines on Steve's face, the kind eyes, and the lips that brought him so much heaven.

"Do you really think we can do it?"

"I think we can do anything if we put our minds to it. I think you can do anything," Steve said. He opened his arms and pulled Scott into a warm embrace, and kissed him softly. Scott closed his eyes and lost himself to the comfort of the hug. All of a sudden, things didn't seem so bad.

"I was so afraid of losing you too," Scott said.

"You don't have to, okay? You don't have to," he said. There they remained, sitting in the darkness, holding each other. It had been traumatic for Scott, but at least he could cling onto this. At least he hadn't lost everything.

Chapter 3

The following week or so was hectic. Scott spent as much time with Steve as time allowed, but his schedule was mainly taken up with packing and arranging things for his move. He'd been on the phone with a representative from his new team. Speaking with her put his mind at ease, for they seemed excited that he was joining them, and they were taking care of everything as best they could.

The closer it got to his move the more nervous Scott was though. He was leaving his home, everything he had ever known, and his relationship for this. It was a huge move, especially for someone like Scott, who had rarely ever left his home state. At night he tried to think about his new life and becoming a success, but it was difficult to shake the habit of a lifetime. Usually when he went to bed he thought of himself lifting trophies wearing the white and black of his home town team, not in yellow and gold.

The initial pain of the news had subsided into a dull ache, but the pain was still there. As much as he had resigned himself to this new status quo he would have done anything if Coach had come in and told him there was a chance he could stay. Perhaps it wasn't fair to his new team, but he couldn't very well change the way he felt.

He endured a final family dinner with his mom and sister.

"Your father would be so proud of you," she said, looking tearfully at his picture that rested on the mantel. "I remember the two of you going out to play hockey, going to games. It's always been your whole life. He'll be cheering you on, and we'll be coming as often as we can to watch you play. You just keep in touch though, okay? Don't you dare be a stranger."

"I won't mom, I promise," Scott said. Most of the dinner was awkward, with his mom talking emotionally about Scott's father and childhood. It wasn't as though Scott needed more pain. It had been years since his father had died, and Scott wished he was still around so he could have given him some advice.

But Scott was alone now.

He even had to fly to his new home alone, as Steve was busy with work. His mom was there to see him off at the airport, and it felt surreal to get on that plane, to feel himself rise from the ground as though he were ascending into heaven, and then to leave for pastures new.

There was no telling what he would find in this new place, or what he would accomplish. Nerves churned and coiled within his stomach. He'd never known life away from the comfort zone of his own home, and it felt as though he was being thrown into the deep end. It remained to be seen if he was going to sink or swim.

The flight was only a short one, and when they approached his new town he peered out the window, intrigued. From his vantage point he could clearly see that this new place was a lot smaller than his old one, and instead of lush forests surrounding the city there were long expanses of desert and plain fields. It was going to take some getting used to.

He got off the plane and gathered his bag. It was such a small airport that there wasn't really a crowd, and he easily spotted someone holding a sign that said his name.

"Scott!" she yelled, waving her arm. From her voice he knew her to be the representative he had spoken with on the phone, her name was Samantha. She looked to be about as young as he was. He smiled at her and shook her hand.

"How was the flight? Welcome, by the way, I'm glad you made it in one piece. Is there anything you need? Would you like to go out for dinner or do you just want to go to your apartment?"

Scott blinked, taken aback by the speed at which she spoke.

"I think I'll just head to my apartment, I could do with freshening up," he said.

"Rightio!" she cried, and led him to her car.

"The whole team is excited that you're here. It's really something. I think Coach wants you to stop by later on so you can meet everyone."

"Sure thing. Remind me again, what's the coach's name?"

"Ray Burr," she said.

"Thanks. Sorry, I'm still getting used to this. My mind is a blur."

"Oh, don't worry, I totally get it. But you're going to love it here. This place is hockey mad and we all really believe we can do some great things this season. Especially now that we're getting a player like you."

Scott shifted uncomfortably in his seat.

"What do you mean a player like me?" he asked, almost afraid that there had been some terrible mix-up and they had thought they'd be getting an actual superstar.

"Let's just say that you're going to be bringing the average age of the team down by about, oh, a century," Samantha said, giggling. "Don't get me wrong, we have a great team, but for the past few seasons we've had a regime of buying old and selling low. It's not really sustainable. We've been getting a lot of veterans to come here, and it's become a joke. People call us the retirement home. There's been a significant change in stance. I think finally people are realizing that we're not going to be able to carry on this way forever so we're getting some young blood in, and it's all beginning with you!"

"Oh, I didn't realize..." Scott said, unsure of how he felt about being a trailblazer.

"It feels like the beginning of something new around here, like there's a new energy in the air. It's all so exciting!" Samantha said. Thankfully for Scott she was happy enough chatting away. As she drove him through the city she pointed out a few landmarks, and a few spots she suggested he shouldn't go. Scott listened with interest, although his mind was thinking about the team as well. He hadn't realized that all of them were going to be older, and he wondered how they would feel about a young guy coming in. Samantha seemed to intimate that the entire town was on board with this new philosophy, but Scott had to wonder how true that was.

Samantha drove him to his apartment and helped him with his bag. He walked in and was impressed. This team really had gone all-out for him.

"It's nicer than my old one," he said.

"I'm sure it'll start feeling like home soon enough. We took the liberty of stocking the fridge. The wi-fi and cable are active, you've got a PS4 there as well and Netflix all set up. I've left a list of numbers and addresses you might find handy, and there's a DVD of our last few games. I've also left a booklet about the club so you can get used to being around here," she said.

"Wow, you're really on top of things," Scott said, impressed.

Samantha blushed a little. Her red hair fell across her cheek, which she brushed away with one hand. Scott dumped his luggage down and stepped into the apartment. It was like a luxury hotel suite. Anything he could think of had been provided for him, and he was starting to feel more at ease with the move.

"I really enjoy my job, and I want to help where I can. This place, it's kinda defined by its sports teams, but they haven't done all that well over the past few years. The recession hit us bad you know, and it's taken us this long to recover. But never say die," she said, putting her fist in the air. "That's our motto," she explained after Scott looked at her blankly.

"Ah. Looks like I have a lot of homework to do," Scott said.

"You know, for a new signing you don't seem to know much about the team you're signing for," Samantha said, folding her arms across her chest.

"I've been meaning to, it's just been hectic. I hope you don't mind me saying, but this isn't the way I saw my career heading. I was a hometown boy you know? There was only one club I wanted to play for."

"I get that, but you have to understand that this is a hometown club for the people of this town, and we like to see our players as devoted as us to the course. It's going to go a long way if you make the effort to be a part of our little world."

"I know, and I will. I've just been trying to wrap my head around this move. It's the first time I've ever lived away from home, or even been away from home. I never really went on vacations, we couldn't afford it. Most of my trips were just spent away with my father. He's the main reason why I got into hockey in the first place. We were always playing together."

"Well you know, we can get tickets for your family anytime, maybe even arrange a tour?"

"Thanks," Scott smiled, "but that's okay. My dad would have been the only one who really wanted to see it, and he's not around anymore."

"I'm sorry to hear that. My dad left too when I was young, and he's the reason why I got into hockey."

Scott offered a sympathetic smile. "My dad died. Cancer."

"Oh my God, I'm so sorry," Samantha said. An awkward silence descended upon them. Scott turned away from her, looking at his new home, suddenly missing his father terribly.

"Well, look, I'll leave you to get settled in. If you need anything my number is on there, or just e-mail me. I'm pretty much at your disposal," she said. Scott nodded at her, and she spun on her heels to leave. But just as she had her hand on the door she turned back. "Scott, sorry, I know this might seem a bit weird, and maybe I'm crossing a line that I shouldn't cross, but as you've seen this is a pretty small town and I don't usually get a chance to meet people who I have a lot in common with who are also around my age. Anyway, I was just wondering if, well, if maybe you'd want to grab a coffee or something?"

Scott turned to face her, the words having barely registered with him as he had been lost in thought.

"Oh Samantha, that would be great, but just as friends, if you don't mind..." It was always awkward when a girl asked him out.

"Oh...of course, sorry," Samantha said, flustered. Her cheeks burned red, and she'd evidently gotten the wrong end of the stick.

"No, wait, I didn't mean it like that. I'm gay," he said.

"Oh. Oh!" she said, smiling with relief. But then concern crept across her face.

"What's wrong?" he asked.

"No, it's nothing," she said, but Scott could tell that she was hiding something. He looked at her expectantly. Samantha's shoulders sunk and she exhaled deeply. "I didn't know you were gay."

"Well, it's not exactly something that I advertise. It's just who I am."

"That's all good and all, but just a word of warning, you might want to keep it on the down low. Like I said, this place is small, and it's...traditional. People around here don't tend to like things they're not used to. That goes for the general public and the guys on the hockey team as well."

Scott's heart sank.

"Great," he said.

"Don't get me wrong, they're great guys, they're just a little, well, backwards in their thinking. You know what the locker room is like. You must have dealt with this before?"

"I have, and I've mostly just kept it to myself, but that's out of a personal choice, not because I've been worried about my safety."

"Well, maybe you'll be the one to change their minds. All I'm saying is don't chuck it in their faces," she said.

"Thanks for the warning," Scott said dryly. With that, Samantha took her leave, and Scott was left alone in his brand new apartment. He had everything there to entertain him and make him feel at home, but he was without the most important thing; Steve. Scott tried to call him a couple of times, but it was only later that Steve got back to him. They had a session on Skype. It was good to see Steve's face again. Even though they had only been apart for about a day Scott was still feeling a schism between them. Being on Skype was fine, but it wasn't the same as being able to rest his head on Steve's shoulder, or take Steve's hand in his. It felt like a shadow of the real thing, and Scott was already wondering how long it was really going to last.

Chapter 4

Scott spent the rest of the day looking at the research material Samantha had provided. He leafed through the booklet and tried to retain as much information as possible about the team and the town, although the only thing that stuck in his mind was the last thing she had said.

It was the 21st century. People were supposed to be beyond this petty bullshit. Scott had always been fortunate, in that he'd never been bullied or ostracized for his sexuality. When he'd realized he was gay, he had told his father, for they had always had a very open relationship. His father had been understanding, and as he grew up it just became something that was a part of him. When people at school asked him why he wasn't interested in a girl, he simply told them that he was gay, and that was the end of it. There had been moments of awkwardness in the locker room and the showers, but that quickly passed, and Scott was never made to feel like there was anything he had to hide.

Until now.

It seemed as though this new part of his life was going to be harder than he anticipated.

Still, he was here now, and he tried to remember what Steve had said to him. Scott couldn't control what had happened, but he could control how he reacted. From what Samantha had said, and from what he learned from the material she had provided, the team was in serious need of some energy. They had a lot of talented players, but their best days were behind them, and the team was in danger of being left behind. There were rumors that a number of other young, hungry players were going to be brought in, and to Scott's dismay there was some consternation from the older players that they were being shut out.

Along with everything else that had been left for him, there were a set of car keys on the kitchen counter. Scott arched his eyebrow and walked down to the parking lot, pressing the button until he found his sleek silver car. He got in and enjoyed the feeling of the plush leather seats, and then made his way to the rink, where he was going to meet his new coach and his new team.

The rink was in the heart of town, and was resplendent. Samantha hadn't been lying when she'd said sports were the lifeblood of this place. They may not have had a lot of money, but what they did have was focused on these temples. Scott pulled into the parking lot and walked around to the corporate area. He'd been in enough rinks now to know the general layout, and soon found his way to the reception desk. He was taken back through the winding corridors of the rink to the Coach's office.

Scott found the idea of meeting the whole team quite daunting, so he was pleased to see there were only two people in the Coach's office. One of them was the coach himself, Ray Burr. The other was Tony Marconi, who Scott would have known anywhere. Tony was the captain of the team, a legend of the sport, and one of his inspirations growing up. As a matter of fact, Scott had been amazed when he looked through the roster at how many names he recognized. Some of the players he couldn't imagine were actually still playing given their ages.

"Scott, it's a pleasure to meet you," Tony said. Tony was the embodiment of masculinity. He was a huge man with broad shoulders and a dark, thick beard. Ray Burr was short and stocky. He was chewing gum, and when he spoke the words burst out of his mouth like bullets from a machine gun. Ray nodded to him and shook his hand as well, then gestured to a seat by his desk.

Scott sat down.

"It's a pleasure to have you here," Ray said. "Are you settling in alright?"

"Oh yes, it's fantastic. I'm really grateful for this opportunity, and everything you've done for me. The apartment is just...it's got everything I could have asked for, and the car is just amazing," Scott said.

Tony chuckled a little. "I remember when I got here the only thing they gave me was a coupon for free wings."

Scott's cheeks flushed, a little embarrassed.

"Yes, well, I don't agree with all this buttering up, but it seems to be the way the world works," Ray said gruffly. "But what I want to make clear to you is that it's not going to be easy for you here. I expect you to work hard to get in the team. I pick players based on merit, so if you have an ego I expect you to chuck it at the door. There's no place for that. It may not look like much compared to where you came from, but we're proud of this team, and we want to do our best for this town. Is that clear?"

"Yes Coach," Scott said.

"Good," Ray replied. "Now then, our scouts were impressed with your showings, and we're glad to be able to give you the opportunity to get you some game time to realize your potential. As long as you give us everything you have, you'll be alright."

"Thanks Coach, I plan to. I want to make sure you know that you haven't made a mistake," Scott said.

Ray leaned back in his chair and nodded to Tony.

"There are a couple of other little things we wanted to talk to you about," Tony said. "I'm guessing you've heard some of the things that are said about this team."

"I...I'm not sure what you mean," Scott said, not wanting to offend anyone by repeating what Samantha had told him.

Tony grinned. "There's no need to be shy around us. We hear it all the time, that this place is a retirement home, that we're just cashing our checks while we can. The thing is, a lot of the players here only know hockey. That's why they're holding on so long, some of them maybe a little longer than they should have. We need some fresh blood, but not everyone is going to like it. We have a few deals in place for some other players to strengthen the squad, but I just want to warn you that you may be met with some resistance. Not everyone is as open about wanting to help the team as we are, but if you have any problems come to me, okay? I've got your back."

"I appreciate that, and I will," Scott said.

"And the other thing is kinda along the same lines. We know there's a generation gap here, and it's our job to try and bridge that gap. We've grown up in different worlds, but we all have hockey in common. These guys are a fount of knowledge. Use that. Frankly, I think that's going to be our big advantage this season. We have the experience and the skill, but all we've been lacking is a bit of zip around the ice. You and the other new players are going to bring that, but the rest of us aren't ready to hang up our skates yet. Learn from us, we're not dinosaurs."

"Got it," Scott said. "Can I just say that it's an honor to play with you and the others. I mean, I know I probably shouldn't say this, but I watched you guys play all the time. Me and my friends used to pretend to be you whenever we played."

"Oh God," Ray said, putting his face in his hand. Scott glanced at him, instantly realizing that he'd said something wrong.

"Let me give you some advice," Tony said, putting a beefy hand on Scott's shoulder. "Never say anything like that again."

Scott began to protest, but Tony raised his hand to silence him. "Believe me, we do not want to be reminded of our age. We're reminded of that every day as our joints creak. If you want to do well here then just treat us as the team, don't treat us as legends. We're well aware we're old. We don't need you to remind us of it," Tony said.

"I'm sorry," Scott said.

"It's okay. I appreciate the sentiment, but there are a lot of guys here who won't look so kindly upon it. Now then, there's someone I want you to meet," he said. Ray nodded toward them, and Tony led Scott out of the office down towards the gym.

"I didn't mean to be harsh on you back there. I get that this is all new to you, I'm just trying to give you some advice that will make this all go more smoothly. Keep your head down, let your hockey do the talking, that's going to be the best thing you can do."

Scott nodded. Every dressing room had its own dynamics, but this one seemed to be more unique than the others he'd experienced. It shouldn't have been a surprise though. It was strange enough for him to be in this place, he couldn't imagine what it was like for people like Tony Marconi, who had been at the top of the sport, and were now not much more than punchlines.

Walking into the gym was like walking into the hall of fame. Everywhere Scott looked there was someone he recognized, and he had to force himself not to stare. Tony greeted everyone and introduced Scott. Some people came to shake his hand, others preferred to just nod. Some barely acknowledged his presence at all.

They walked past the exercise equipment and went into the massage parlor. A deep moan greeted Scott's ears. There was a shaggy-haired man laying on the massage table, with the masseuse standing over him, pressing the heels of his palms into the man's flesh. Scott was stunned by how handsome this masseuse was. He had a radiant aura about him. He was more slender than everyone else in the gym, which set him apart (Scott had never really liked the muscular jock look anyway) and when their eyes met it was as though a lightning bolt struck Scott.

"Scott, this is Mark, he'll take care of any twinge you have. He's the best in the business," Tony said.

Mark shook Scott's hand. Scott felt the oil slide against his skin, but underneath there was warm flesh. The smile between them lingered, and then a flush of guilt lanced through his heart as he thought about Steve.

Then Tony introduced him to the man on the table, Lee Bowers, another legend of the game, and the man who played in the same position as Scott.

"So, you're the guy who is after my spot," Lee said as he pushed himself up. He brushed his thick hair away from his face, showing a toothless smile. His body was covered in hair.

"I'm just here to play hockey," Scott said.

"Yeah, well, I ain't going down without a fight. This is bullshit and you know it Tony," Lee said. He rose from the table and wrapped a towel around his waist, then stormed out of the room. Scott wasn't sure what to think.

"I'm sorry about that, let me go and talk to him," Tony said, leaving Mark and Scott in the room together.

"So, you're the new hotshot everyone is talking about," Mark said with an easy smile.

"I wouldn't go that far," Scott said.

"People have been raving about you around here. They reckon you're just what this place needs," Mark said. "I mean, I'm 33 and I'm younger than most players on the team."

"I just hope I can do my part. Although I guess not everyone is pleased to see me," Scott said, glancing back at the door through which Lee had stormed.

"Ah, don't worry about him. A lot of the guys here are frustrated that their bodies aren't doing the things they're used to being able to do. I can understand it, it must be hard when the thing you've trusted the most starts betraying you. Try not to take it personally. It's not you they hate, just the march of time. They know it's been coming for a while, but now it seems like it's the twilight of their careers for most of them. Not that you'll be hearing me say that to their faces, and I'd suggest you to do the same," Mark said.

"Yeah, Tony told me something along those lines already."

"Tony is one of the few who has his head on straight. He knows the score, that he can't do it forever. A lot of them though, like Lee, well, hockey is the only thing they know. Being out on the ice, that's their whole life. They grew up in a different time. Now, people are more prepared for the future. They know it's a short career, but when Lee and the others were playing they thought the gravy train was never going to stop."

"It's weird for me to see them like this."

"You'll get used to it. They're just men, like the rest of us," Mark said. But Scott was quickly starting to think that Mark wasn't like most other men. He had an easy manner about him, as though nothing would ever bother him. Scott hoped the two of them could become friends.

"How are you settling in?" Mark asked.

"Okay so far. It's my first time away from home, so I'm still processing everything."

"It's going to take you a while. Soon enough you'll wonder why it took you so long to leave though. There's nothing like the feeling of independence."

"It's not the independence I'm afraid of, it's leaving behind everything I used to know."

"Yeah, I get that. Well look, if you get tired of hanging out with the players feel free to give me a call. I'm usually around to hang out," Mark said, offering him his number, which he wrote down on a scrap of paper. Scott took it and stuffed it in his pocket and thanked the man. Scott felt as though he was getting definite vibes from Mark, but it was difficult to trust himself at this moment. His emotions were all over the place, and he was afraid that he was just transferring his feelings for Scott onto Mark.

At that point Tony returned and apologized for Lee's outburst. He promised they wouldn't all be like that, and then took Scott away to meet the rest of the team properly, and to be shown his place in the locker room. But, for the entire time he was meeting everyone else, Scott couldn't stop thinking about Mark and his winning smile, his easy manner, and the mischievous twinkle hiding in his eyes.

Chapter 5

The first couple of weeks of pre-season passed pretty quickly. Scott had settled into his apartment and was beginning to feel like part of the team. A few other new signings had joined, and the atmosphere in the locker room was a little tense. The older players felt as though they were looking at their replacements, and it only served to remind them that their time as hockey players was winding down. Each of them reacted differently though. Some of them took the younger players under their wings. Scott wasn't so lucky. Lee had a huge chip on his shoulder and didn't cut Scott any slack. He always went hard on him in training, and more than once Scott ended up bruised.

But his way to the first team was much clearer than it was at his old club, and he was actually beginning to feel excited for it. The only thing missing from his life was Steve. The distance was difficult to deal with. Phone calls, Skype calls, and texts just weren't the same. It also didn't help that he wasn't able to talk about it with anyone on the team thanks to Samantha's warning. Still, Scott was determined to make it work, and was already making plans to bring Steve down for a visit.

Some of the things he most looked forward to were his massage sessions with Mark, and not just because of the physical relief they brought him. Mark was so easy to talk to, and these sessions were just about the only time when Scott didn't feel incredibly lonely.

"Another battering from Lee today?" Mark asked when Scott stripped down to his underwear and lay on the table. His body was covered in bruises, some of them fresh, some of them fading.

"You know it," Scott said.

"I can hurt him back for you if you'd like, I mean, I know which nerves to press to cause him a great deal of pain," Mark offered. Scott chuckled.

"I think I'll be okay for the time being," Scott said, "but thanks for the offer."

"How are you doing now anyway? Are you starting to think of this place as home yet?" Mark asked. The two of them continued talking while Mark lathered up his hands with oil and began to rub Scott's flesh, easing out the tension that built up in the muscles, getting deep into the tissue.

Mark was a genius with his hands, and it was only now that Scott realized how amateurish the massages he'd received before were. Tony hadn't been lying when he said that Mark was the best in the business. The man made Scott's body feel alive in a way that it never had before. His body tingled as Mark's hands and fingers ran over the naked flesh. At some points it felt as though Mark's hands were everywhere, undoing the knots that had twined in Scott's back, releasing tension in his legs. It was amazing, electric, and totally inappropriate.

Every time after it was over Scott chastised himself for being so weak. Then he told himself that it was harmless, and he was just enjoying a little physical attraction that was being denied in his relationship. But it wasn't as simple as that. He genuinely looked forward to spending time with Mark, and almost wished that he had more issues with his muscles so that he had an excuse to see Mark even more, in a professional setting.

Because of his attraction, he hadn't yet taken Mark up on the offer of meeting for a drink. Scott was afraid of what might happen. He was already feeling tense because of his absence from Steve, and Scott didn't want to put himself in a position where he might make a fool of himself. Especially because he didn't want word to get out among the rest of the team that he was gay.

Thankfully, Mark wasn't insistent. He told Scott stories about the team and the things he'd had to endure over the course of his career, and Scott often found himself shaking with laughter. The massage table felt almost like a therapist's couch, and Scott found himself talking about things he wouldn't usually share with anyone else, like memories of his father, and how scared Scott had been to come to this place. In fact, the only thing he didn't talk about was his relationship with Steve, and he felt guilty for keeping this part of him from Mark, when really he should have been frustrated that he couldn't spend this time with Steve.

Scott knew that if he didn't do something soon this cocktail of emotion would rip him apart, and he'd end up doing something stupid. Mark's massages always left him aroused and in need of relief, but his own hand wasn't proving to be effective enough. So it was that later that night Scott called up Steve on Skype, wanting to arrange a date.

They exchanged pleasantries as the call began, and Scott was relieved to see Steve's face. His hair was tousled and he looked a bit dazed, as though Scott had just woken him up.

"What's up?" Steve asked.

"Nothing much. I just missed you," Scott said.

"I miss you too. It's not the same here without you," Steve said.

"I know what you mean. I'd really like for you to come down and see me. Maybe you can catch the opening game of the season? I don't know if I'll be starting, but I think I'll get on the ice at some point," Scott said.

"I might be able to, I'll have to check with work first, but they do owe me some time," Steve said.

"There's just one thing if you do come down though..."

"What's that?" Steve asked warily, taking note of the cautious tone in Scott's voice.

"When you do come down, we have to keep things on the down low. It's not like home. People aren't so open-minded. Nobody on the team knows about me."

"Oh for Christ's sake! Are you kidding me? What the hell are you talking about? What kind of place are you living in?"

"It's just that people here are quite traditional and I'm new, so I don't want to go rocking the boat. The guys on the team are already wary of me and I don't want to give them another reason to push me away. We can still be together here, just if we're at the rink..."

Steve shook his head and pinched the bridge of his nose. "Scott, you shouldn't have to do that. What are you thinking? You should be proud of who are you."

"I am proud! I'm just trying to make my life a little easier. I know it's not perfect, but I really miss you. It's not the same sleeping alone. I need to feel your body next to mine. Please, can you just come down and visit? If I have my way we won't be leaving my bed much anyhow," Scott said with a teasing smile.

Steve was just about to answer when suddenly the bathroom door opened and a shirtless guy appeared on screen. He was well-built, and a towel hung around his waist. As soon as he appeared Steve angled the camera away, but before he did Scott saw the guy duck back into the bathroom with a clearly surprised look on his face.

"Who the hell was that?" Scott asked.

"That was just Ricky, from the office. He's having girlfriend troubles so he asked if he could crash."

"In your bed?" Scott asked.

"Come on Scott, it's not like that," Steve said, but Scott knew Steve well enough to know when the man was lying. Scott's heart broke in his chest. He could feel the shards pressing against his skin. His head went light, and everything felt as though it was spinning.

"Scott, please, just hear me out, it's not what you think. It doesn't mean anything. You know how it is...how lonely things get," Steve said.

"I know Steve, I know," Scott choked, and then ended the call. He tossed his phone across the room, ignoring the vibrations. Steve was calling him again and again, but Scott knew there was no coming back from this. The long distance thing wasn't going to work. While Scott was here struggling with his own desires, Steve was indulging his. It was a brutal betrayal. Scott buried his face into the pillow and beat his hands against the mattress.

Everything in his life had fallen apart and there was nothing he could do about it. For the sake of his career, he had to be the poster boy for a new era for this team, even though he had no emotional attachment to this town, and now he was truly alone. Even though he was a part of the team he didn't feel a part of the brotherhood. There was nobody he could call right now...nobody except Mark.

Scott glanced across the room at the phone. It was late, but Mark had made it clear that Scott could call him any time and he would answer. Scott scrambled over and picked up the phone, swiping away all the alerts and the messages that had come from Steve. There was nothing left of that anymore.

As soon as Mark had given him his number Scott had put it into his phone, but was yet to have called it. He had always been afraid, but there was nothing holding back that fear now. He needed to speak to someone about this, and everyone else he knew were miles away.

Before he could second-guess himself he pressed the call button and heard the dial tone. Mark's voice answered.

"Hey, it's Scott."

"Oh Scott! Wow, it's late, what's up?"

"I was just wondering if you wanted to go for that drink?"

"Uh, yeah sure," Mark said, and they arranged a meeting place. Scott wiped the tears from his eyes and splashed some cold water on his face. He wasn't going to let Steve ruin what was left of his self-esteem. He wasn't going to let this betrayal break him, but he also wasn't going to be able to hold in the truth for much longer. He had to talk to someone, and he could only hope that his instincts about Mark were right, because if he was wrong, if Mark wasn't trustworthy, then it could cost Scott his career.

Chapter 6

The two of them met at a sports bar. There were a few groups in there, but it wasn't very busy. It only sounded like it because of the noise these groups were generating. Mark welcomed him with a smile and offered him a drink. Scott noticed how good he smelled, fresh, like a summer's breeze.

"Don't take this the wrong way, but you look like hell," Mark said. "Talk to me about it."

"I'm not sure if I should," Scott said, suddenly afraid of being out and about. Paranoia was taking hold of him and all he could think about were the horror stories he'd read about other people in his position who had been victimized for their sexuality.

"Why not? I can't believe you called me up this late just to shoot the shit," Mark said. "Whatever it is, I promise you it'll stay between the two of us. Call it masseuse-patient confidentiality."

Scott laughed at this, and was put instantly at ease.

"Okay, but I'm going to take that as a verbal contract and if anything bad happens because of this it's going to be considered binding by my lawyer," Scott teased back. Mark smiled and dipped his hand into the nuts on the table, letting them fall into his mouth before he took another swig of his drink.

"Well, go on then, talk to me," he urged.

Scott took a deep breath. He was hunched forward, and was turning the glass around and around. He took a long sip and then looked at Mark.

"I've heard that people around here are traditional," Scott began.

"I guess that's true for the most part," Mark said.

"Well, I'm not exactly a traditional guy," Scott said.

"Okay...I'm not really understanding what you're getting at here."

"I'm not what people think I am. I've got a secret."

"Well, everyone has their secrets."

"I know, but if this one gets out it could spell trouble for me, and I don't want trouble, but I really needed to speak to someone and you're the closest thing to a friend I've got here. Although you're part of the team you're not really on the team, so I'd like to talk to you about this, but I don't want any word of this getting back to anyone else," Scott said. So far Mark had been pretty casual about the whole thing, but now Scott's serious tone was making him worried.

"Scott, honestly, you can trust me. As long as this isn't something to do with you murdering someone you can believe me when I say that I won't tell anyone. You can trust me. We are friends. Please, tell me what's on your mind."

"My boyfriend and I broke up. I'm gay."

"Oh, is that it?"

Scott gave him a questioning glance.

"Sorry, I didn't mean to be insensitive, it's just that I knew you were gay."

"You did?" Scott asked, looking around warily.

"Well, yeah, just like I'm sure that you know I'm gay."

"You're gay?" Scott asked. A thrill surged through his body, in some ways he had always suspected, but had put it down to wishful thinking and his own frustrations.

"Well, yeah, but anyway, what happened between you and your boyfriend?"

"We'd been dating for a few months before I came here, long enough that we were both committed. At least, I thought we both were. We decided to do the long distance thing and I tried to get him to come down here for a visit. It was hard being away from him, but apparently too hard for him. We were talking on Skype and then some random guy came out of the bathroom wearing one of Steve's towels."

"That's pretty damning. I'm guessing there's no other explanation?"

"He tried to tell me it was someone from his work but I know everyone he works with, and it was written all over his face. He couldn't be patient. He couldn't just hold out for me."

"Well, that sucks. He should have been honest with you if it wasn't working for him. Some people are just annoying. I guess now is the point where I trot out all the clichés about you being better off without him."

"I guess, not that they ever make anything better."

"No, they don't. I'm sorry that happened."

"I'm not even that mad at him, which is the main thing. I'm more mad at myself that I didn't see it, and that I don't really have a support network here."

"Well, you've got me. And I know how hard this is. I remember the first time I fell in love. I was with this guy at school. He was amazing. He said he wanted to keep it on the down low because he wanted it to be special, something just for us. I thought he was sweet, until I eventually found out that he was saying the same thing to a bunch of other guys. Some people just get off on the attention. Frankly, it's better you found this out now rather than when you had poured more of yourself into the relationship. Sorry, that was getting into cliché territory again."

"I'll let that one go," Scott said. He felt instantly better just for being in the company of Mark, and found that actually a lot of the hurt dissipated quickly. He was already more interested in what Mark had to say than dwelling on the betrayal of Steve. Perhaps it was the long distance that helped with that, Scott told himself.

"So what's your story? How do you be a gay man in a place as traditional as this?" Scott asked.

"You know, it's not as hard as people think. When I came to work here I did a lot of research about the place and it quickly became clear that I would have to keep my head down, but it's no different to when I was back at school. As far as I'm concerned I mind my own business and other people can mind theirs."

"But doesn't it bother you that you can't be yourself?"

"Sure, sometimes, but it's not like I'd be mixing my personal life and my professional life anyway."

As those words left Mark's mouth Scott's heart sank. He exhaled slowly and pressed his lips together. He didn't know what he expected from this night, but part of him hoped that his attraction with Mark would flourish. After all, Steve was able to indulge his desires, it seemed unfair that Scott had to be starved.

"All I'm going to say," Mark continued, "is to take care of yourself. Focus on your hockey and everything else will fall into place. You know, right now I'm guessing everything feels like it's falling apart, and you're struggling to find a constant. The one thing you have is hockey. Use that. And the people on the team, they're good guys. They'll have your back as long as you trust them."

Scott nodded, although he still felt hollow inside. He looked around at the bar. There were a few couples making out.

"Sometimes it makes me sick, thinking that they can just kiss out in the open, but if two guys do it suddenly it's an outrage."

Mark shrugged. "The world is changing, maybe not as quickly as we'd like, but it'll get there."

"So about not mixing your personal life and your professional life, do you never hang out with the team?" Scott asked.

"No, but it's not like I'm asked often. The team is the team, and I'm just a masseuse."

"Then isn't it strange you're here with me?"

"You seemed to be in need," Mark said, a teasing gleam in his eye. There were moments like this when Scott wondered if there was more to this meeting, if there was some chance that Mark could be interested in him, despite what he said about his worlds being separate.

Scott's mind was awhirl. Whenever he thought he was steady, he thought about Steve and that guy again, the two of them in the bed that he and Steve used to share, and his heart broke all over again.

"I am," Scott replied. Do you ever feel like life is just rolling away out of your control and there's nothing you can do to stop it? I mean, when I was younger I used to think that when I became an adult I'd figure out everything that I needed. My dad…he seemed to have it all under control. I guess it just seems that way now."

"Your dad seems to be an important figure in your life."

"He is, and I wish that he was still around. He always knew the right thing to say and do. He never steered me wrong."

"Well, what do you think he'd say if he were here now?"

"Probably much of the same thing you're saying. He'd tell me that a guy like Steve isn't worth distracting me from what's important, that relationships are supposed to enrich my life, not cause problems, and that I can't control what he did to me, but I can control how I respond to it, and it's up to me to decide how much sadness and pain I spend on him."

"That sounds like good advice to me."

"Yeah…I miss him," Scott said, gazing into his drink.

"I bet you do. I'm sorry that he's not around."

"Thanks. I just…I just wish sometimes I could see him again, you know? Even if it was just for five minutes. Just so he could see…just so I could tell him, well, I don't know what I'd say. There's so much."

"I think there's always too much to say. There is never enough time, and you're always left feeling like you should have said more."

Scott's eyes began to glisten with tears. He wiped them away surreptitiously, but Mark saw. Mark tugged at Scott's arm and suggested for them to leave. Scott nodded, feeling numb.

The cool air of the night hit them as they left the bar. There was nobody else in the parking lot, and for the moment it seemed as though it was only the two of them in the world. Scott stumbled along. He wasn't drunk, just desolate because of the turbulent emotions in his heart.

"I'm so lonely," Scott blurted out. He felt ashamed for being so vulnerable, but there was nothing he could do to hide it. Everything was building up inside of him, and if he didn't let these feelings go they would eat him up from the inside. He blinked hard, trying to stop the tears from streaming down his face, but a few escaped. He turned his head away from Mark, not wanting the masseuse to see his pain.

"It's okay to be lonely. It's human. But it won't stay that way forever," Mark said.

"I'm out here, alone, with no family, no friends."

"You're not alone."

"Don't try and tell me that I've got the team, because I can't go to them with any of this."

"I was going to say that you've got me," Mark said, pulling at Scott's shoulder. Scott tilted his head up to look him square in the eyes and was overwhelmed by the kindness and compassion within them. Mark was like an oasis in the desert, a sea of calm in the middle of a raging storm. He exuded confidence and stability, and he was sexier than anyone Scott had ever seen.

Before Scott knew it his instincts had taken over and he threw himself at Mark, pressing his body against Mark's, plucking a kiss from Mark's lips. A fire flared within Scott for a moment, but then Mark pushed him away. There was a look of confusion on his face, and a look of horror on Scott's as he realized what he had done. Ashamed, he fled, even as Mark called after him.

Chapter 7

Scott raced home and flung himself on the bed, feeling utterly hopeless. Mark had shown him kindness and friendship and he'd ruined that by breaking Mark's rules. Mark had made it clear that there were some lines he didn't cross, and Scott had just gone and crashed through them. Scott wailed and tried to find his way through the anger and pain that careened through his heart. In one moment he was sad as he thought about his father, the next he was angry when he thought about Steve's betrayal, and in the next he was scared of the immediate future. There seemed to be no solid ground on which he could stand. Everything was slipping away from him, and he was totally alone.

But then he thought of Mark and he was suddenly filled with confidence and strength. The lingering heat of Mark's lips scorched him, and the fire within felt as though it would burn eternally. His heart thumped and the desire for Mark hardened and smashed the other emotions into submission. Soon enough there was only a pure, burning need for Mark.

Scott's body reacted, stiffened. His hand fell naturally down his body and curled around his swollen manhood. His entire body was on fire and all he wanted was to feel the sweet release of lust. Closing his eyes, his mind was alive with thoughts of Mark and only Mark. Scott relived the tender touch of Mark's hands sliding against his skin. He thought about the musky scent of Mark's aftershave as the man leaned over him and ran his hands all down Scott's back. Scott moaned softly as he squeezed and writhed, tingles shot down his body, small explosions erupted over his skin as his body relived the massages Mark had given him.

There was nothing about them that was supposed to have been erotic. Mark was a professional, as was Scott, but Mark was so gorgeous, and Scott's lust for him so strong, that it was impossible not to think of them in that context. Scott thought about Mark's hand running up his inner thigh, a rush of breath escaped his lips. He stroked and pumped and twisted his head this way and that, wishing it was real, almost being able to feel Mark's skin on his.

The feeling was electric and Scott's body tensed completely. Every inch of him was rigid at the mere thought of Mark, and as the passion built up inside him Scott knew it was going to be glorious. A smile twisted on his face as sweat beaded on his temples. He brought himself closer and closer to a sweet climax, intending to slow down and make the pleasure last for as long as possible, but when the time came to do so he was so aroused, so tempted by the delicious release that he was unable to stop himself. It built up inside him, coursing through the core of his body, and before he knew it his mind cracked and a hot stream covered his thighs, stomach, and hand.

A long groan left his lips as his hand fell limply to his side. Scott was utterly drained, and it felt glorious. For a few moments the heady afterglow of orgasm cocooned him. His glistening chest heaved with deep breaths, and his head lolled to one side. Then, all of a sudden, it evaporated. He looked around at his dark room, his empty bed, and all he could see were shadows. A bitter taste rested on his tongue. He couldn't have Mark. At the moment it didn't seem like he could have anyone.

The only thing he had was hockey. It was clear to him that his career had to be his focus. It hadn't led him in the direction he would have chosen, but he was here, and he had to make the best of it. His dream was still to make it in his home town, and he'd do everything he could to ensure he made it. It was time to put his career first, and his personal life second.

Everything he did at the beginning of the season was aimed toward that goal. He trained hard, harder than most, and set an example for the rest of the squad. Tony praised him for his attitude, but Scott took this with a grain of salt. He didn't need praise. All he needed was to play.

And it just so happened that he was given his first chance in the first game of the season. Lee Bowers was injured after twisting his ankle in training, so Scott found himself in the line up. There was still some resistance in the crowd to the new, untested faces, so Scott lined up alongside all the idols. Some, like Tony, had been impressed with his showing in training, while others only saw the threat Scott and the others posed.

Ray and Tony had been doing a good job at preventing a schism from forming between the older and younger players though. The two of them made it clear that everyone was going to be on the team on merit, and that the only thing that counted was the skill shown out on the ice. Lee, however, glared at Scott, and before the match he came over as Scott was getting ready, standing mere inches away from Scott's face. Scott could smell the stale breath as Lee spoke in a growling voice.

"You'd better not get used to it out there. As soon as I'm ready I'm going to be back on that ice and you'll be where you belong, on the bench." He made a point of jabbing a finger into Scott's ribs. Scott didn't say anything in response. He'd spent too long in the reserves to go back there. He'd been brought here to play hockey, and that was just what he was going to do.

And he was never more sure of that, than when he stepped out on the ice on the first game. Hearing his name being called out gave him a thrill, and seeing the crowd rise and applaud him was an indescribable feeling. The atmosphere was intoxicating, and as soon as the metal blades of his skates touched the ice and he took his position, he understood why the rest of the squad were so reluctant to let go of their careers. There was nothing that compared with being on the ice, nothing that could ever come close to the glorious feeling that swelled within his heart. This was where he belonged. He was a gladiator and this was the arena in which he was going to shine, he was sure of it.

He remembered everything he had learned over his career, starting with the basics his father had taught him at home, carrying on through all the lessons he'd learned after he turned professional. It stood him in good stead. He started nervously, but quickly grew into the game, and ended up winning plaudits. The team won, and although he didn't feel he had played as well as he could, the fact that he was a new player made the press focus on him. All the headlines were about the new era that was being ushered in by the young signings, and since he had been the first, Scott was the face of this new era.

The days and weeks that followed showed a startling change in the way Scott was perceived by those around him. He was invited onto local talk shows and radio shows so the people of the town had a chance to get to know him better. He was becoming something of a local celebrity, and after being in the shadows for so long, it was strange to get used to being in the limelight.

Even though it was difficult to admit, it was impossible to deny that this move had benefited his career. As he lay in bed at night he thought about what his life would be like if he had remained at home. He'd still be toiling away in the reserves, waiting for his opportunity, dreaming of being on the ice. The reality was far greater than the dream, even if he was wearing yellow and gold instead of black and white.

But, for all this newfound fame there was still something missing from his life. Companionship, love, a little romance. Of course everyone assumed that he was straight, and there were plenty of fans who had made clear their intentions toward him. Even on the talk shows he'd had to deflect questions about his private life, and he wondered how long it could go on for.

In his quiet moments he thought of Mark, of the kiss they should never have shared. Mark had offered him friendship and he'd tried to take something else, something more. It hadn't been fair to Mark, and it was something that he couldn't take back.

It had been difficult, but Scott had managed to avoid Mark. Mark wasn't the only masseuse the team had, and whenever Scott needed one he had always worked the schedule so that he saw someone else. But it wasn't the same. Nobody had Mark's magic touch, and Scott couldn't stop fantasizing about Mark. Every night Scott's mind was alive with thoughts of him and Mark together, exploring each other, with Scott attempting to give Mark as much pleasure as Mark gave him.

And every time the pleasure was intense, but the only thing left when it faded was a hollow melancholy. Scott tried to tell himself that hockey was the only thing he needed, but he couldn't fool himself. There was a deep yearning inside him to be close to someone, and he knew he wanted that someone to be Mark.

At first he'd tried to tell himself that his feelings for Mark were just the product of his failed relationship with Steve, that he was rebounding hard. But as the weeks passed and turned into months he was unable to shake Mark from his mind, and it was clear that his feelings ran deeper than a mere rebound. Whenever he thought about Mark his heart skipped a beat, and he wished that he was able to let go of the feelings. He kept telling himself to focus on hockey, that the better he played the sooner he would be able to get his dream move, but it didn't help. Mark had been etched into his soul, and letting go of his feelings for Mark was utterly hopeless.

But while Scott was spending these weeks training hard and playing well, trying to tear away the feelings that were in his heart, he wasn't the only one feeling the turmoil of emotion. Lee Bowers, the living legend, had hatred and anger festering within his heart. Scott was getting all the plaudits, while Lee was being forgotten. His injury had healed, but because of Scott's form he wasn't able to fight his way back into the team. He glared at Scott whenever they were near each other, but Scott was so caught up in his own feelings that he wasn't aware how deep the ire ran.

One day, Lee had had enough. He wanted his spot back, and he was determined to do anything to get it. In training, he targeted Scott, battering into him under the guise of making a good impression on the coach. Scott could tell that Lee was out to injure him, and it took all of Scott's skill to avoid the attacks of the older, bitter warrior. But after training Scott's body showed the signs of wear and tear. He was bruised and battered, and his muscles ached, but he was determined not to let the pain show.

The Coach had other ideas.

"Get yourself down to the masseuse," Ray ordered.

The color drained from Scott's cheeks.

"I really don't think that's necessary," Scott protested, but his words fell on deaf ears. When Ray gave an order he expected it to be followed, so Scott had no choice but to go and get a deep tissue massage from Mark. His nerves rattled at the thought of seeing Mark again. When he opened the door Mark was surprised to see him, but although the eyes were kind the gleam of friendship had gone.

"Coach told me I had to come and see you," Scott said, getting undressed. Mark gestured to the table as he spread oil over his hands.

"Looks like someone did a number on you," Mark said. There was an edge to his words. Scott wished he could take back what he had done outside the bar, but so much time had passed now it just didn't seem possible. Silently, he lay on the table, and let Mark do his job.

Chapter 8

"You're so tense," Mark said as he pressed his elbow in between Scott's shoulders. Mark was working his magic and although Scott wasn't pleased to be here, he was at least grateful for Mark's talents. The pain in his body had subsided a little, and he knew that he would be better off for it in the long run.

"Can you blame me?"

"I guess I can't, not if Lee was out to get me," Mark said.

"How did you know it was Lee?"

"It's hardly likely to be anyone else. I see what's going on, and he's been in here a few times. I know how much he wants to be back on the ice," Mark said. "Although from what I can see he doesn't deserve it, not with the way you've been playing."

Scott's ears pricked up at this. Somehow getting praise from Mark meant more than all the praise he'd received from other quarters. It was strange to be talking with him again, but laying in silence was too awkward, and it wasn't doing anything for the tension that held his body rigid.

"Thanks, but I don't think it's going to stop him from trying," Scott said.

"Well, you've been doing really well. I'm...I'm proud of you," Mark said. Scott furrowed his brow. The way he said it was more than a friend, but he was afraid his mind was playing tricks on him again. Scott felt it best to remain silent. Anything he said could only lead to more trouble.

The massage continued, and although Scott tried to relax he was unable to. Mark continued pressing deep into his tissue. His fingers spread all over Scott's body, working their way over the middle of his back, down his thighs, massaging deep into his calves. His body wanted to release the tension, but his mind wanted to cling onto it desperately. This scenario had been the fuel for passionate fantasies, to be in this room again with Mark was surreal. Scott had to battle against his own mind to not let himself slip into a state of arousal. He'd already embarrassed himself in front of Mark once, he didn't need to do it again.

"Seriously, what is causing all this tension? There are knots all over the place. I don't know what you've been doing with yourself, but this isn't good. You should have come to see me sooner. I don't think I'm actually going to be able to get this all done in the time we have today," Mark said.

"I couldn't," Scott said, glad that his face was looking at the floor. Mark sighed and put his full weight on Scott's back, then took it away.

"I think you should sit up. I don't want to have a conversation with you when I can't look into your eyes," Mark said. Scott reluctantly sat up, shoulders slumped, trying not to make eye contact with Mark because he was afraid of the feelings it would elicit.

"Look, about what happened-" Mark began.

"I'm sorry," Scott interrupted. "I shouldn't have done what I did. I know you have your boundaries, and I broke them. I was just messed up, and I read things into that night that weren't there. You were just trying to be a friend to me and I ruined it."

"I appreciate the apology, but actually I was going to apologize."

"What do you have to apologize for?" Scott asked, confused.

"For pushing you away. I shouldn't have done that. I just wish you hadn't run away. I wanted to talk to you more, explain...but when you started avoiding me I figured that you weren't interested anymore."

"Not interested? No I...I mean, I was just afraid that you didn't want me coming around, that I would complicate your life or something."

"You've definitely done that," Mark said, smirking. He sat down on the table beside Scott and sighed. "But I don't regret it. Look, when I said that I kept my personal and professional life separate I meant it, but I didn't mean to imply that it was a hard and fast rule. What you told me really stuck with me. To be honest, part of the reason why I keep these parts of my life separate is because I'm looking for a relationship and romance, not a fling, and in my experience athletes aren't the type of men that I like being in a relationship with. I like my men to be emotionally available, and you proved that you are. You're not like anyone else on the team, and I like that. I wanted to try and tell you that, but you were so busy playing, and I didn't want to put you off your game. Plus, given that you had just broken up with your boyfriend I wondered if you were just looking for a rebound thing."

"I wasn't," Scott said tersely.

"I guess we're both a victim of miscommunication here," Mark said, trying to lighten the mood.

"I feel like an idiot."

"You are, a little bit, but that's not always a bad thing," Mark said, nudging Scott with his shoulder. Scott's frown gave way to a smile, and he shook his head as he chuckled. "There, that's a little better. I can see the tension already lifting from your body."

"I can think of another way for that to happen," Scott said, leaning in tentatively. Mark mirrored his movements. The two men tilted their heads to lean into each other, and a soft, tender kiss followed. Scott's heart opened at the touch of Mark's lips, and he was overwhelmed with a feeling of ease and calm. All of his anguish dissipated, scorched away by Mark's kiss.

Their lips pressed against each other and their breaths curled, melting into each other. Mark's hand came up to the back of Scott's head. His fingers twined through Scott's hair. Scott's hand fell to Mark's thigh, squeezing it gently. Scott shuddered as the kiss grew deeper. Their mouths opened wide and they thrust their tongues out, ready to dance together. A soft moan escaped Scott's lips as he found himself leaning back, until he was on the massage table again, but this time with Mark laying on top of him.

Scott was in a world of delight. His right leg hung off the end of the table, and Mark completely engulfed him. The older man kissing him firmly, with great hunger, and it seemed as though both men had been deprived of this kind of genuine affection for a long time. More than that, Scott could feel Mark's arousal pressing against his thigh. Heat rose within and he knew exactly what he wanted, for they had to make up for lost time. Scott reached down and groped Mark's ass. Mark buried himself in the nape of Scott's neck, and tingles began to spread all over Scott's body, willingly succumbing to a state of delirium.

A haze grew over his mind and he began to lose himself. Mark became everything to him, and the rest of the world melted away.

Until the door opened.

"Oh fuck me," Lee said, rubbing his hands. "I thought you were taking your time Mark. This is very interesting indeed."

Chapter 9

Scott pushed Mark off him, for both their sake. If this came out both of them could be in a lot of trouble. Lee smiled with glee, relishing the moment. An incandescent fury raged within Scott. He stood up, pushing the masseuse table behind him with the force of the momentum, and clenched his hands into tight fists.

"I think I'll skip my massage today, I'm suddenly feeling a lot more relaxed. I think I've just had a problem taken care of," Lee said.

"Get out of here Lee, this is none of your business," Scott growled.

"Oh I quite agree, but it is the business of the team. I think they should know that one of their own is lying to them. I bet the both of you have loved it haven't you, you perverts. You get to look at us in the shower, probably feeding your midnight thoughts, and you," he turned to Mark, "you make me sick, having your hands all over us. I bet you jerk off after every session."

"It's not like that," Mark said, trying to be reasonable.

"Maybe, maybe not, but what will people think? They like their wholesome family fun around here. Do you think the team will ever trust you again? The fans? Your career here is ruined," Lee said. It was clear he enjoyed the thought of it. "It's been nice knowing you."

He turned and walked out of the office. Scott and Mark glanced at each other. Scott was terrified. He chased after Lee, even though Mark was shaking his head. Scott caught up with Lee halfway down the corridor and pulled him back.

"Whatever you're thinking of doing, don't," Scott said.

Lee glared at him. "You think you can tell me what to do? Fuck you man, I don't need this shit. You want to fuck guys, go ahead, but this is the end for you here."

Scott anxiously looked around, but there was nobody to hear them.

"It doesn't have to be this way. Mark could get fired, and you know there's nobody as good as him. Do whatever you like to me, just don't let this fall back on him."

"I bet you'd like me to do whatever I like to you," Lee said, baring his teeth in a malicious smile. Scott's stomach churned at the thought. "The thing is Scott, I don't owe you anything. The truth is going to come out, and it's going to be glorious. I don't care who gets burned by it." Lee turned away from Scott again and took a few steps before Scott hurried to walk up to him.

"Okay, okay, how about this. How about you don't tell anyone at all?" Scott said. In his mind he saw the uproar from the fans and the rest of the team. He saw the headlines. Even though the world had moved on from a lot of prejudice, the arena of sports was a grim exception. Rarely had any athlete come out as homosexual, and in this area Scott wasn't sure he wanted to be a trailblazer.

"And why would I ever do that?" Lee asked, holding back a laugh.

"Think about what this means for you. Do you want to get your place back because of a scandal, or do you want people to think you got your place back because you earned it?" Lee narrowed his eyes, wanting to hear more. Scott tensed his jaw and inhaled deeply, not really able to believe that he was going to say this, but he knew he had to for the sake of his career, and Mark's. It was one thing for himself to take the fall, quite another for Mark's life to be disrupted. "I'll...alter my performances. You'll get your place back, just don't say anything, please," Scott pleaded.

"You'll have to make it look real. I don't want anyone thinking I'm getting charity," Lee said.

"It'll be real, I promise," Scott said.

"Okay, but if I ever think that you're not doing as you promised I'll tell everyone what I know," Lee said, jabbing a meaty finger threateningly towards Scott. Scott gulped and nodded, then turned back to talk with Mark.

"It's taken care of," Scott said, closing the door behind him. His voice was hollow, and all the electric passion that had built up inside him had evaporated.

"What did you do?" Mark asked.

"I told him that he could have his place back if he didn't tell anyone."

"Scott..."

"I had to do it. If he told everyone you'd lose your job and I have no idea what would happen to me."

"It might not be that bad."

"It would, and you know it. They might not even really care all that much about us being gay, but they'll sure as hell care that we lied to them. You know what some of them would be like with you, having been touched by you over the past few seasons. Not all of them are going to think it's innocent. And I'm sure that if you asked any of them they'd say they didn't have any problem with homosexuals, as long as they don't shove it in their faces. I knew I should have turned tail and ran as soon as I found out what this place was really like."

"Is that what we do now, we run?" Mark asked. He was still perched on the massage table, having returned it to its rightful position after Scott had inadvertently pushed it aside as he rose to meet Lee. Mark's hands were clasped together and he spoke in a low, thoughtful tone. "Is that what all of our progress has come to? God, I hate this world sometimes."

"Me too, but what else can we do? Do you want to out ourselves and risk our careers?"

"I don't know, maybe."

"Well, if we do, we have to be damn sure of it. It won't be so bad. Lee won't be around for much longer. All I have to do is wait out a season or two and he'll retire, then things will be back to normal."

"And what about us? Scott, when I think about us being together it's not hiding behind closed doors. I guess that's one of the reasons why I've been single, because I want to be open. I don't want to have to hide myself, or my feelings."

"You might be ready to risk your career for this Mark, but I'm not ready to risk it for you. Lee won't do anything as long as he gets what he wants. And the thing is, if the truth does come out, I might just survive because I'm part of the team. I'm the face of the new era. People won't want to let that go so easily. But you? You're only a part of the background. The fans don't have any attachment to you, and where does that leave us? You'll be somewhere else, and there's no guarantee that I'll be able to get traded to wherever you go. We'll be left with nothing, and I'd rather have you here."

Scott walked over and took Mark's hands in his.

"It's going to be okay, we just have to be a little patient," Scott added. Mark looked up at him. There was a lot of anger and pain in his eyes.

"I get what you're saying, I do, but I've seen this happen before. It never ends well."

"What do you mean?"

"When I was younger, there was a guy at high school. I got caught with him and they threatened to out us. We decided to hide it. We said that we could carry on the way things were and just keep to ourselves, but it wasn't that easy. We couldn't just be ourselves. We were so paranoid that everyone else knew, and to be honest they did. Even though the secret wasn't out people knew that something was wrong, and it didn't take them a lot of guesses to figure out what. It tore us apart you know, and we never recaptured that early feeling of intimacy. We stopped speaking to each other because we couldn't handle the looks we were getting, and it came to a point where it was just easier to deny everything. I have a feeling the same thing is going to happen here. Sure, we can see each other, but as long as we're worried about people finding out there's always going to be some tension between us, and it's going to cast a shadow over whatever we're doing."

"It won't be like that. I promise. As long as I stick to the deal we won't have any problems from Lee. I'll just have to put my career on hold for a season or two."

"That's the other thing. I don't want you to have to do that," Mark said. "It's not fair. You're only just coming into your own, and you're doing great. Your career is going to be short enough as it is, you don't need to make this sacrifice for me."

"I know I don't have to, but it's my choice Mark. I can't let this hurt the both of us," he said, placing his hand across the side of Mark's face. He wrapped his arms around Mark and the two of them embraced. Scott leaned down and kissed the top of Mark's head. Scott tried to convince himself that it was going to be okay, but there was a nagging voice inside him that told him he should listen to Mark.

The two of them decided to keep a low profile for the following few days, just to make sure that Lee wasn't going to say anything. Scott was continually berating himself for this happening though. It always seemed like one thing or another had to stand in the way of his happiness.

Chapter 10

The following few weeks were just about the most difficult of Scott's career. He did as he had promised Lee. In training he stepped down a gear, and in games he made errors until Ray had no choice but to drop him. People were mystified about his recent drop in form, but he had no explanation. He became withdrawn, almost becoming mute when he was on the rink, and the frustration festered inside him.

Acting like this, was going against everything his father had taught him, and it pained him to think how ashamed his father would be of him. He tried to tell himself that he was doing it for Mark, but even the moments they shared together were brief and clandestine. It always felt as though there was some spark missing from them, and they both knew the source of it. Scott was on edge, and he was reading another report in the local paper about his drop in form.

"Sometimes I wish they did know the truth," he said, flinging the paper across the room. Mark sat on the sofa in silence.

"Would it be so bad?" Mark asked. Scott glared at him. Ever since this had first happened the two of them had become increasingly testy with one another. There were some points when Scott wondered if the two of them would even be dating if they weren't under this shared umbrella of misery.

"We've talked about this," Scott said.

"Maybe it's time to talk about it again," Mark replied.

"What more is there left to say?"

"Plenty, I think. A lot has happened over the last few weeks. I hate to say I told you so-"

"Then don't say it."

"Fine, but I warned you this would happen. Let's be honest with each other Scott, is this the way either of us hoped we would feel? Is that what you imagined us being like when you thought of us together? This thing hangs over us like a shadow, and I'm finding it difficult to enjoy this romance."

Scott had always known that one of them was going to say it, and once it was said it couldn't be taken back.

"Do you want to break up?" he asked meekly.

"No," Mark said, "at least I don't think so. I just want...I want to date the guy I was first interested in. I told you before that I don't like emotionally unavailable men, and for the past few weeks you've been withdrawn. You're not yourself, and I know it's because you're having to hold yourself back on the rink."

"I did it for you."

"Yes, but I never asked you to, so don't go blaming me. You wanted this."

"I never wanted any of this! All I wanted was to be happy," Scott said, his voice cracking under the weight of emotion.

"Then let's do all we can to be happy," Mark said. The two of them had been sitting on opposite ends of the couch. Mark moved over to the floor, sitting in front of Scott, an imploring look in his eyes. "Scott, this isn't working, and I don't think it's going to work until you get back on that rink and play to the best of your ability."

"But if I do that we could lose each other. We could lose everything."

"Haven't we basically done that already? When you get up in the morning do you look in the mirror with pride? Do you actually look forward to going to work? Because I sure as hell don't. I'm always afraid now that Lee has told someone, and they're looking at me differently, and I'm scared because I don't want your sacrifice to be in vain. But I can see that this has taken the joy of hockey away from you, hell it's taken the joy of life, and when we get to that point is it even worth keeping the secret any longer? Is the alternative going to be that much worse?"

"I don't know," Scott said simply. He sighed, and then leaned back on the couch, resting his eyes. He put his hand across his forehead and massaged his temples. "You're right, I do feel like I've lost myself. The worst thing is that I feel like I've failed my father. I know he wouldn't want me to be acting like this, but it's like I've gone too far down a hole I've been digging, and it's easier to tunnel through to the other side rather than climb back up."

"It doesn't have to be."

"What do you suggest, that I just come out?"

"I think it might be time for that, yes. Turn the tables on Lee. Tell everyone what really happened. He definitely doesn't deserve to come out of this with everything he wants. He's getting a hero's send-off when he should be the one ashamed of himself. I just hate seeing you like this. The spark that I fell for just isn't there. You're not the man I know you can be."

Scott groaned inwardly when he heard this. It felt as though everything had crumbled around him and he didn't know where to begin picking up the pieces. All he wanted was to do the right thing and make the right decision, but no matter what he did he felt as though he was being led down the wrong path.

"Scott, please don't let this ruin you. You're too good at hockey, you're too good a man to be defeated by this. All I know is that something has to be done, because I can't see us going a year or two like this. I can't see you doing it either. You're not happy, and it seems obvious what has to happen for you to be happy."

"But how am I supposed to go and do that? I've never been one to want my whole life out there, exposed."

"Sometimes we don't have any choice. Maybe it's for the best this way anyway. Maybe what this town needs is for people to stand up and tell their truth. Think about it Scott, we can't be the only ones struggling with these hidden desires. People shouldn't have to be afraid of judgment. This could be an important step. They said that you're bringing a new era to this team, well maybe you should live up to that in more ways than one. I'll be right here by your side no matter what happens, but I have a feeling that it won't be as bad as you initially thought."

"You really think so?" Scott asked skeptically.

"I know you don't want this burden, but sometimes you have to be brave out here as well as out on the ice. You didn't ask for this, but I think it might be time to show people who you really are."

Mark was sitting beside him. He rested his hand on Scott's thigh. In this apartment the two of them could be alone, hidden away from the world, but Scott knew Mark was right. He'd lost himself recently, both on the rink and off it, and unless he did something drastic he was going to find it more difficult to get back. In his heart he new that Mark was right. He knew what he had to do, and in the back of his mind his father's voice was telling him to go for it.

"I suppose it is."

"Do you know what you're going to say?"

"No, but I know what I want to do right now," Scott said. With a mischievous gleam in his eye, he launched himself forward and pinned Mark to the floor, kissing him passionately.

"Now that's more like it," Mark said, grinning.

Scott breathed in deeply. Now that he had made the decision to confront the truth he felt much better about himself, and more like the man he used to be. The fire that had dimmed over the past few weeks was burning brightly again, and it was ready to tear the world asunder. But first, there was much he had to do with Mark.

Scott enveloped Mark in his arms and drowned him in a kiss. Scott's muscular body rippled with tension and desire stormed through his veins. Mark was equal to him, however, and began clawing and groping at his back. The two of them rolled across the floor, tearing at each others' clothes. They only paused to gaze into each others' eyes before they kissed passionately again.

Heat rose within Scott's mind and the world grew hazy. Strength coursed through his body and he felt as though he could conquer the world. He throbbed with desire, and as their bodies were locked together he could feel that Mark's body swelled as well.

Scott rose from the floor and tore his shirt over his head. He was in the process of unbuttoning his pants when Mark ran up and tackled him, pushing him against the wall. They kissed like crazy. Mark had Scott's arms pinned above his head, before Scott used his strength to reverse their positions and slam Mark against the wall. Mark dragged his fingers down Scott's body and tasted his bare flesh, while Scott was still struggling to get Mark undressed.

The two of them found their way to the bedroom, and Scott threw Mark onto the bed. Mark lay there seductively before he reached out his hands and pulled Scott by the waist of his pants toward him. Mark had a hungry look in his eyes as he groped at Scott's jeans, fumbling with the belt frantically until he pulled it away and tossed it aside. He grabbed the thick bulge and Scott felt a warm surge flow through him. Mark eagerly stripped Scott, and then began to play with his manhood, which was as impressive as the rest of his physique.

Scott stood there and ran his hands through Mark's hair, enjoying the pleasure that Mark was giving him as he made love to Scott with his mouth. Scott watched every inch of his cock disappear into Mark's mouth, then reveled in the sight of Mark's saliva glistening on his manhood. Mark closed his eyes as he opened his mouth and took Scott again and again until Scott felt the tension surging through his body, but he wasn't ready yet, so he stopped Mark and pushed him to the bed.

"Let's not rush things. You're not even undressed yet," Scott said. He pulled Mark's top over his head, and then fell to his knees, running his hands through the thick bed of golden hair that ran down Mark's torso. The hair narrowed into a thin line past his navel, leading to a wondrous delight.

Scott fell to his knees in between Mark's legs and began to stroke his thighs, pulling away his pants. Mark's black boxers were stretched to their limits. Scott peeled them away slowly, and smirked when Mark's long cock sprung up. Scott rubbed his hands all over the long shaft, then bowed his head and began pleasuring Mark just as Mark had pleasured him. He sucked eagerly, and enjoyed feeling the pressure of Mark's hand against his throat. Scott pumped with his hand as he sucked, and felt his warm drool slip down, making everything wet and moist. As he sucked he slipped his fingers down to explore the dark, sweet spot that caused Mark to moan loudly. Scott looked up with his eyes, loving how he could control Mark's movements with just one curl of his finger.

"Oh my God," Mark said, the words rushing out of his mouth like a gushing waterfall. His face contorted with pleasure and his fists fell either side of him, clutching the sheets of the bed.

A muffled moan escaped Scott's lips, his mouth was filled with cock so he couldn't speak. The heat washed over his body and he enjoyed the bitter taste and the musky scent of Mark. He buried himself in Mark's groin and let the spirit of Eros wash over him.

"I need you. I fucking need you. Fuck me you fucking god," Mark said desperately. Scott was all too happy to oblige. He rose and wiped the drool away from his mouth before he spit on his hand. Mark crawled back up the bed and turned around. Scott spat on his hand, making it nice and wet and crept up behind Mark. He reached out his left hand, rubbing Mark's rump, feeling the tensed muscles, and with his right he prepared Mark, making him nice and wet.

Then, Scott positioned himself and slipped inside Mark slowly and gently, loving the tight feeling that enveloped him. The two of them soon became one, and once Scott was inside he leaned his head back and let out a guttural cry of glory. With both hands on Mark's hips, Scott began to thrust, falling into a gentle rhythm at first, before a crescendo of passion crashed through him and he was seized by a need to be as deep inside as possible.

The hot air was filled with their grunts and moans. Scott leaned forward, letting his hands roam all around Mark's body, while his erection drove deep into Mark. Scott's body was flooded with pleasure.

He reached around and found Mark's erection, and held it tightly, letting the motion of their two bodies jerk Mark off. Both men shuddered and shook. It felt as though the whole world was being tormented by an earthquake. All the tension that had been building up for the past few weeks was being released, and Scott was feeling like a phoenix rising from the flames.

His torso dripped with sweat. His muscles were sculpted like a Greek Adonis. Pleasure swam through his blood and his mind cracked with the sheer force of his desire.

"I'm coming. Oh my God I'm coming," he breathed.

"Come in me baby, give me everything," Mark grunted, and Scott obliged. The two men surrendered themselves to a tidal wave as Scott released himself, all the tension instantly draining away. Mark was at the height of his orgasm as well, and his shuddering body only added to Scott's pleasure. The thick jet of cum burst over Scott's hand, and the warmth trickled along the side of his palm to his wrist.

Scott pulled himself away and lay down on the bed, his chest heaving.

"That was..." he began.

"Everything I've been waiting for," Mark finished. The afterglow of love hung over them like a starry sky, and after they had washed they held each other closely, their naked bodies as close as two physical forms could ever be.

"Do you still think you can go through with this?" Mark asked.

"For you, I can do anything," Scott said, kissing him tenderly before the two of them fell asleep.

Chapter 11

Scott had been thinking about what he was going to say for a long time. The closer the moment grew, the calmer he felt, which surprised him. Once he had made the decision to go public a feeling of serenity had come over him. It was as though he had been warring with himself in trying to keep this a secret, and the moment he decided to do something about it he felt much better. There was still much that was to be decided. He didn't know how people were going to react to his news, but he knew that Mark was right, he couldn't live with this hanging over him for the next two seasons. He wanted to be out on the ice, and if people couldn't accept him for who he was then he'd find somewhere else to play.

He'd called a press conference to tell the town the news, and all the local outlets were there, many of whom he had spoken to when he first arrived. These were the same people who had been questioning his recent form. Tony and Ray had asked him what was going on, but Scott hadn't told them anything.

Just before the press conference Lee came up to him and stood in front of Scott, blocking the sun.

"You'd better not be doing what I think you're doing," Lee snarled.

"What does it matter to you?"

"It matters. You think if you come clean people are going to understand? You're going to be hung up like a pariah," Lee said. "If you want to throw your career away then go for it, you'll be giving me exactly what I want."

The fact that Lee was worried only made Scott more sure that he was doing the right thing. Before he went into the press conference he heard his father's voice in the back of his mind as well, telling Scott that he was proud.

Scott took a deep breath and entered the press conference. The gaggle of reporters quietened down when Scott strode to the podium, sitting alongside Ray and Tony. Before he spoke to the assembled guests, he leaned over and quickly apologized for the secrecy.

"I hope that once I'm finished you'll understand, and I won't hold your reactions against you," he said. Ray and Tony looked mystified.

Scott then turned to the gathered throng and smiled at them.

"Thank you all for coming today. I know there have been some questions about my recent form, and I'd like to use this forum to address some of those concerns," he took a deep breath. This was it, and he had their full attention. "I have been playing below my ability, and I'd like to apologize to the fans and the rest of my team for that, but please hear my explanation.

My father always told me that I should never be afraid of myself, and that I should never be ashamed of who I am. I've tried to live by those words my entire life, but since I've come here I haven't been able to. You see, I'm gay, and I know that may come as a surprise to a lot of you. It might even disgust some of you. Someone found out and threatened to use it against me. Out of fear I allowed him to get what he wanted, thinking it was the best for my career. But I quickly came to realize that I had no career if I wasn't able to be myself, I had no life.

There are some things that are more important than hockey and careers. Personal well-being is at the top of that list, and while I was denying myself, feeling ashamed of myself, I wasn't happy at all. It took a special person to show me that it didn't have to be that way, that I didn't have to live in fear.

I'm coming to you today with this because I want to send a message to everyone. It's okay to be yourself. You shouldn't have to be ashamed. My father gave me these lessons a long time ago. I strayed from them, but I've come back to them, and I hope that wherever he is now, he's looking down on my with pride. I know there are other people struggling with trying to fit in, with having to feel like they have to pretend to be someone else. I'm here to tell everyone that they don't. I don't know what's going to happen to me. I have disrespected myself, this team, and this town by not playing to the best of my ability, but I hope that you will all look at yourselves and the people around you and show a little more understanding. Don't let them live in fear of your judgment. Make it clear that they can be themselves.

That's all I really have to say. Thank you for your time," he said.

There was a moment of silence as the people present processed the news, then suddenly there was a barrage of questions. Scott was overwhelmed with them, and he was looking in every direction, unsure of who to answer first, before Tony put a hand on his shoulder and stood up.

"I want everyone here to know that Scott has the full backing of myself and Ray. A lot of this is an internal matter for the team to deal with, and there are a few things we're going to have to talk about," he said, staring pointedly at Scott, "but as for him being gay, I want him and everyone to know that anyone is welcome on this hockey team as long as they give it their all. Now, I have a feeling why this happened, but I'd like to go on the record to you all and say that if you don't support Scott in this, then you don't support the team, and you should take a long hard look at yourself."

There were flashes from cameras as Ray took the microphone from Tony.

"I'll back what my captain said," the gruff Coach barked. "The only thing that matters to me is the performance on the field, and it's the only thing that should matter to the lot of you as well. The personal life of my players should not be under scrutiny. Everyone is entitled to live their lives how they want to, as long as they're not bringing harm to anyone else, and I just hope that we can all put this incident behind us and get back to focusing on what happens on the rink again," Ray said.

He and Tony nodded to Scott. Their support and approval meant a lot to him, although Scott knew that he still had much to make up for. He whispered a thank you to both of them, but Ray made it clear that if he ever gave less than 100% again he would be off the team quicker than the road runner.

The team's press officer, who by this point looked as though he was going to have a heart attack, shuffled Scott and the others away to field the questions. As soon as he was away from the glare of the media Scott glared at Lee, but he didn't rat him out, even though Tony had a good idea who was responsible for all this.

"All I want is to play hockey," Scott said, and that was good enough for Ray and Tony.

Scott gave his all in training that day and he felt much better for it. He was finally letting himself loose, and it felt as though he was flying after his wings had been clipped. After training he ran back to Mark and told him the good news.

In the days that followed, the press conference went viral, and people were commenting on it all over the country. Some weren't complimentary, but Scott received many messages of support, and it led to a lot of other people being brave enough to speak about their own feelings and their own struggles. Soon enough even other well-known hockey players were coming out, and it seemed as though a few dominoes had fallen.

But the messages of support that meant the most, were those from his mom and his old coach. They told him how proud they were of his actions in talking about his feelings like this, and how it was wrong that anyone should have used his personal desires against him. And when Scott stepped back on the ice he received a standing ovation. The whole crowd held signs showing their support, and although the opposing players tried to use it to get under his skin, the rest of his team wouldn't let anyone say bad words against him.

Scott was finally happy, and all it took was to accept himself. At the time it seemed far easier said than done, but all it had taken was a risk. Just one risk, and he had everything his heart desired. His relationship with Mark went from strength to strength as well, now that he had shed himself of his doubt and shame. He even started to reconsider his thoughts about a dream career. Of course it would be nice to represent his home town team, but what was more important was playing, and making the man he loved proud.

Mark was there at every game, cheering him on, and Scott knew that life couldn't get any better. His life certainly hadn't gone where he'd wanted it to. The dreams he'd had as a child hadn't come to fruition, but he was happier than he'd ever imagined, and he'd come to understand that sometimes it was better to let life flow naturally rather than fighting against the tide.

In time, he came to accept his new town as his home and forged a life he was proud of. He and Mark were like two peas in a pod and Scott had never been happier than when he was with Mark. The entire club proved to be supportive of him, and even the players who showed disgust at his lifestyle were soon silenced by his performance on the rink, which got better and better as he became more settled.

Through it all, Scott remembered the example his father had set, and was finally convinced that he had grown into a man his father would be proud of. Indeed, he had turned into a man who was proud of himself. Scott had brought a new era to the town, but it was a new era for his life as well. Letting go of the anguish of the past, Scott developed a new sense of confidence and enjoyed thinking about the future, both professionally and personally. He went from strength to strength, earning accolades and plaudits from fans and pundits alike. He became more of a cult hero in this place than he ever would have had he stayed at his boyhood club, and Mark was there standing beside him every step of the way.

*****

Don't miss out!

Visit the website below and you can sign up to receive emails whenever Van Cole publishes a new book. There's no charge and no obligation.

https://books2read.com/r/B-A-RTRV-QZZIC

BOOKS 2 READ

Connecting independent readers to independent writers.

Also by Van Cole

3 Man Huddle: MMM Best Friend Romance
His Alpha Wolf: Gay First Time Romance
A Dragon's Miracle: Gay Dragon MPREG Romance
Double-Teamed: MMM First Time Football Romance
His Football Star: Gay Second Chance Romance
Love In My Town: MM First Time Romance
Training A Hockey Star
Game Night
Double Shift
Take A Shot
Dear Professor
Getting Inked
Ninth Inning
Triple Threat
Seducing My Best Friend's Brother
My Protector
The Blueprint
Show Me The Way
End Zone
Matched To His Tiger
Love At First Puck
My Straight Boss
Falling For The Alpha
My Boss
On Thin Ice